A Note to Parents and Caregivers:

Read-it! Readers are for children who are just starting on the amazing road to reading. These beautiful books support both the acquisition of reading skills and the love of books.

The PURPLE LEVEL presents basic topics and objects using high frequency words and simple language patterns.

The RED LEVEL presents familiar topics using common words and repeating sentence patterns.

The BLUE LEVEL presents new ideas using a larger vocabulary and varied sentence structure.

The YELLOW LEVEL presents more challenging ideas, a broad vocabulary, and wide variety in sentence structure.

The GREEN LEVEL presents more complex ideas, an extended vocabulary range, and expanded language structures.

The ORANGE LEVEL presents a wide range of ideas and concepts using challenging vocabulary and complex language structures.

When sharing a book with your child, read in short stretches, pausing often to talk about the pictures. Have your child turn the pages and point to the pictures and familiar words. And be sure to reread favorite stories or parts of stories.

There is no right or wrong way to share books with children. Find time to read with your child, and pass on the legacy of literacy.

Adria F. Klein, Ph.D.
Professor Emeritus
California State University
San Bernardino, California

Editors: Jacqueline A. Wolfe, Christianne Jones
Designer: Joe Anderson
Page Production: Lori Bye
Creative Director: Keith Griffin
Editorial Director: Carol Jones
The illustrations in this book were created with acrylics.

Picture Window Books
5115 Excelsior Boulevard
Suite 232
Minneapolis, MN 55416
877-845-8392
www.picturewindowbooks.com

Printed in the United States of America.

Library of Congress Cataloging-in-Publication Data
Blackaby, Susan.
Allie's bike / by Susan Blackaby ; illustrated by Shawna J.C. Tenney.
p. cm. — (Read-it! readers)
Summary: After putting on safety gear, Allie is ready to learn to ride her new bicycle.
ISBN-13: 978-1-4048-2403-4 (hardcover)
ISBN-10: 1-4048-2403-0 (hardcover)
[1. Bicycles and bicycling—Fiction. 2. Hispanic Americans—Fiction.] I. Tenney,
Shawna J.C., ill. II. Title. III. Series.

PZ7.B5318All 2006
[E]—dc22   2006003440

Allie's Bike

by Susan Blackaby
illustrated by Shawna J.C. Tenney

Special thanks to our advisers for their expertise:

Adria F. Klein, Ph.D.
Professor Emeritus, California State University
San Bernardino, California

Susan Kesselring, M.A.
Literacy Educator
Rosemount–Apple Valley–Eagan (Minnesota) School District

PICTURE WINDOW BOOKS
Minneapolis, Minnesota

Allie put on her pink helmet. She put on her white elbow pads and knee pads. She hopped on her new red bike. She was ready to go!

Her bike tipped this way. She leaned to the side.

Her bike tipped that way. She leaned to the other side.

Her bike tipped over. Allie tipped over, too. She tipped into a bush.

Bike riding can be tricky.

Allie tried again.

Her bike wobbled this way. She wobbled to the right.

Her bike wobbled that way. She wobbled to the left.

Her bike wobbled over. Allie wobbled over, too.

She wobbled into the garden.

Allie tried again and again. And then,
a funny thing happened.

Allie got better and better!

Now Allie's bike zips. She zips past her friends.

Her bike zooms. She zooms past her dog, Bones.

Allie zips and zooms on her new bike.

More *Read-it!* Readers

Bright pictures and fun stories help you practice your reading skills. Look for more books at your level.

The Bath 1-4048-1576-7
The Best Snowman 1-4048-0048-4
Bill's Baggy Pants 1-4048-0050-6
Camping Trip 1-4048-1167-2
Danny's Birthday 1-4048-2408-1
Days of the Week 1-4048-1581-3
Eric Won't Do It 1-4048-1188-5
Fable's Whistle 1-4048-1169-9
Finny Learns to Swim 1-4048-1582-1
Goldie's New Home 1-4048-1171-0
Jake Skates 1-4048-2412-X
The Lazy Scarecrow 1-4048-0062-X
Little Joe's Big Race 1-4048-0063-8
The Little Star 1-4048-0065-4
Meg Takes a Walk 1-4048-1005-6
The Naughty Puppy 1-4048-0067-0
Paula's Letter 1-4048-1183-4
The Tall, Tall Slide 1-4048-1186-9
The Traveling Shoes 1-4048-1588-0
A Trip to the Zoo 1-4048-1590-2
Wendell the Worrier 1-4048-2425-1
Willy the Worm 1-4048-1593-7

Looking for a specific title or level? A complete list of *Read-it!* Readers is available on our Web site:
www.picturewindowbooks.com